CONTENTS

Page No.

Red Riding Hood — 7

Cinderella — 33

Hansel and Gretel — 59

Sleeping Beauty — 85

Text by Maureen Spurgeon

My Treasury of
FAIRY TALES

Brown Watson

ENGLAND

Red Riding Hood

There was once a girl called Red Riding Hood. That wasn't really her name, but her dear grandmother had made her a red hood and cape, rather like those which ladies wore under their hats when they went out riding. And so, Red Riding Hood was what everyone called her.

Now, Red Riding Hood was a nice little girl, always cheerful and kind. So, when she heard that her Grandma was ill, she asked if there was anything she could do to help.

"Well, Red Riding Hood," said her mother, "I'd be glad if you could go and take some food to Grandma and see how she is. But it would mean you'd have to go through the wood!"

"Oh, I don't mind!" cried Red Riding Hood. She was thinking how nice it would be to stroll through the wood, and maybe pick some flowers for Grandma on the way.

"Well," said her mother again, "you must promise to go straight to her house, and no dawdling! Remember not to stop and speak to anyone you don't know!"

Now, Red Riding Hood really did mean to do what she had been told. But it was all too easy to forget, especially with the sun shining and so much to see on the way.

It was all so quiet, she had no idea that anyone else was there.

"Little Red Riding Hood . . ." murmured the wolf, seeing the red cloak. "She'd make a fine supper . . ."

"Good day, Red Riding Hood," he said with a friendly bow. "May I ask where you are going?"

"To Grandma's cottage," she said. "On the other side of the wood."

This set the wolf thinking.

"Why not take a short cut along this path, my dear?" he said, knowing very well that the way he pointed was twice as long . . .

But his idea was to get to the
cottage long before Red Riding
Hood. Then, he thought, he could
eat up poor Grandma, as well.
What a feast he would have!

Still panting a little, the wolf knocked on Grandma's door.

"Who is there?" she quavered.

"It's me, Grandma," replied the wolf, in a voice as sweet as he could make it. "Red Riding Hood."

"Oh, Red Riding Hood!" cried Grandma in delight. "Lift up the latch and come right in."

And, with a loud roar, that wicked old wolf burst into the cottage!

Poor Grandma fainted at once, but before the wolf could take the first bite, he heard the sound of a gun outside. Best put the old woman in the wardrobe, he decided.

The sound of guns told the wolf
that hunters were about, and the
wolf did not like hunters one bit!
Besides, he thought, Red Riding
Hood would be arriving soon . . .

So he put on Grandma's nightcap and gown and got into bed. Soon, a soft voice called, "Grandma! It's Red Riding Hood!" "Come in, dear!" cried the wolf.

"Oh, Grandma!" exclaimed Red Riding Hood, as she came up to the bed. "What big eyes you have!"

"All the better to see you with!" murmured the wolf.

"But, Grandma!" Little Red Riding Hood said again, "what big ears you have!"

"All the better to hear you with," growled the wolf.

Red Riding Hood began to think that something was very strange . . .

"But, Grandma!" she said for a third time, "what big teeth you have!"

"All the better to EAT you with!" roared the wolf, and he leapt out of bed. He reached out to grab Red Riding Hood with his long, powerful claws!

Red Riding Hood began to scream, and this made her poor Grandma bang on the wardrobe door. The wolf roared again, not knowing that the hunter he had heard was right outside . . .

He kicked the door open and strode into the cottage, raising his gun. He had been hunting the wolf for a long time — as that cowardly beast knew only too well!

With one last, desperate roar, he dashed out of the cottage, determined to escape the hunter's gun for the last time. After that, he was never seen again.

By this time, Red Riding Hood had heard the banging on the wardrobe door, and let her Grandma out. And how glad they were to see the last of that wicked wolf!

But, Red Riding Hood began to cry.

"It's my fault," she sobbed. "I should have done what Mummy told me, and not spoken to the wolf."

"Well," smiled Grandma, "I'm sure you won't do it again, dear."

"Now," she went on, "let's all have some tea. Then our friend the hunter can see you safely home."

Cinderella

Once, Cinderella and her father, the Baron, had lived alone, after the death of her mother when she was a baby. She loved him dearly.

How she sighed, remembering those happy days before her father married a widow with two daughters of her own.

The widow's daughters were so ugly and cruel, that they quickly became known as The Ugly Sisters.

Soon, the Baron's daughter was made to do all the house-work.

She was dressed in rags, and
because she spent so much time in
the kitchen among the cinders,
they called her "Cinderella".

Then, one morning, Cinderella
heard a loud knock at the door.
   It was a message from the royal
palace, sent to all the houses in
the kingdom.

"Invitations to a Grand Ball in honour of the Prince Charming" squealed the Ugly Sisters.

Cinderella's heart began to beat.

She ran up the cellar steps, almost bumping into the Baron! "Father!" she panted, "the invitations that have come for the Grand Ball! I can go, can't I?"

But before the Baron could answer, Cinderella's step-mother shouted out:

"You? Go to the Ball dressed in your rags? Talk sense, Cinderella! You're only fit to stay at home!"

Cinderella knew the Baron was too afraid of his wife to say anything. The Ugly Sisters were delighted, glad of an excuse to make Cinderella work harder than ever.

"Alter my dress!" "Brush my hair!" "Shine my shoes!" "Iron my gloves!"

They meant to look their very best for the handsome Prince Charming.

By the evening of the Ball, Cinderella was so unhappy she could hardly bear it. Alone in the house, she sat by the fire, her tears falling into the cold, black cinders.

Then, a dazzling glow of light seemed to fill the kitchen, making it bright and warm.

"Do not cry, Cinderella", came a soft voice. "I am here to help you."

"H – help me?" Cinderella stammered. "But, how? Who – who are you?"

"Your Fairy Godmother," came the reply. "And with my magic wand, I shall see that you go to the Ball!"

Before Cinderella had time to answer, her Fairy Godmother gave a tap with her wand — and, in an instant, her rags became the most beautiful ball gown she could ever have imagined!

"I shall need a pumpkin . . ." said the Fairy Godmother.

"There is one in the kitchen garden . . ." said Cinderella.

The Fairy Godmother turned a fat pumpkin into a lovely crystal coach! Four mice became white ponies, and two rats were changed into footmen!

"Thank you, Fairy Godmother!" cried Cinderella.

"Just remember my magic can only last until midnight!" her Godmother smiled.

What a stir there was when Cinderella arrived at the Palace! Everyone wanted to know who the beautiful young girl was — including Prince Charming, who at once came up to her.

They danced together the whole evening, falling in love with each hour that slipped by.

The Ugly Sisters had no idea that the very beautiful girl was Cinderella!

On the first stroke of midnight,
Cinderella remembered what her
Fairy Godmother had said.

"I — I have to go!" she cried, and
she turned and off she ran down
the stairs.

Prince Charming was
surprised and knew he had to
see the beautiful girl again.
The only clue she left was a
tiny, glass slipper . . .

There was great excitement
next day. A fine royal procession
came around all the streets, with a
page carrying the glass slipper on
a red cushion.

"Whoever this slipper fits," said the Royal Herald, "shall marry Prince Charming!"

"It will fit me!" squealed the first Ugly Sister. "It will fit me!"

"No, me!" screamed her sister. But, the slipper was much too small for either of them.

"But, this is the last house!" cried the Herald. "Is there nobody else?"

"Only my daughter," said the Baron quickly. "I'll call her."

And even before he put the slipper on Cinderella's tiny foot, the Prince knew she was the girl he loved.

Soon, Cinderella and the handsome Prince celebrated their marriage. And somewhere, Cinderella knew, her Fairy Godmother was there, smiling.

Hansel and Gretel

In a wooden cabin at the edge of a thick, dark forest, there lived a poor woodcutter and his wife. They had two children — a boy named Hansel, and a girl whose name was Gretel.

Times were very hard, and more often than not, there was barely enough to eat.

"We cannot go on like this, wife!" said the woodcutter, one night.

"And what about the children?" she sobbed. "Suppose we die before they do? Who will look after them?"

"We could always leave them in the forest one day," said the woodcutter. "If we do that, at least they will have nuts and berries to eat. And noblemen out hunting might find them and give them a home."

Next morning, there was only a crust of bread for the two children to share before they all set out for the forest. Only little Gretel saw Hansel putting it into his pocket...

Then Hansel crumbled the bread, ready to drop a piece every few paces as they went through the forest. Now, he thought, they could find their way back home!

After they had gone quite a
distance, the woodcutter made a
fire to keep the children warm.
Stiff and tired, they laid down,
hardly caring where they were.

Next thing they knew, it was completely dark!

"We're lost!" Gretel kept crying. "How can we see the pieces of bread to guide us home now, Hansel?"

On and on they walked
through the forest, their feet
becoming blistered and sore.
Suddenly, Hansel stopped. "Look,
Gretel! Smoke coming from a
chimney!"

Gretel could see nothing. But as they came nearer, the children saw a funny-looking cottage with a pretty little garden, and flowers that sparkled like sugar candy!

"Mmm, delicious!" cried Gretel, picking a leaf. "Try some, Hansel!" But he was already taking bites of sponge cake tiles and wondering if the marzipan roof tasted as good!

Suddenly, they heard a voice,
cracked and wheezing.
"Who is there? A little mouse?
Who is nibbling at my house?"

It was the ugliest old woman
they had ever seen! Gretel turned
to run, but the woman spoke
kindly.

"Hungry, are we? Come inside,
I've plenty of food to spare!"

Hansel and Gretel had never seen such a meal! How could they have guessed that the kind old woman was really a witch who lay in wait for children?

"A pity they are so thin," she cackled to herself as they slept. "Still, that makes the boy light enough for me to lock him up in my cellar without any trouble!"

Early next morning, Gretel was awoken by a hard kick.

"Get busy, you little wretch!" screamed the witch. "Fetch some water and light the fire!"

73

Gretel was too frightened to disobey.

"You can cook a meal for your brother," the witch went on. "I want him fattened up before I eat him!"

And every day, the witch came to see how fat Hansel was getting. "Let's feel your arm," she would scream. Hansel always held up one of the bones Gretel passed to him.

Luckily for Hansel, the witch could not see further than the end of her nose.

"Too thin!" she would screech. "Still too thin!"

At last, the witch decided she could wait no longer.

"Girl!" she screamed. "Stoke the fire and get the oven hot! Fat or thin, I mean to eat your brother!"

Hansel was amazed to see how
calmly Gretel began to obey the
witch.

"Please," she said after a while,
"will you check to see if the oven is
hot enough?"

The witch dashed forward at once, rubbing her hands greedily. And the moment she put her head inside, Gretel pushed as hard as she could — and slammed the door shut!

With trembling fingers, Gretel unbolted the entrance to the cellar.

"Come out, Hansel!" she cried. "The witch cannot harm us, now!"

But Hansel refused to leave the cottage without taking as much of the witch's treasure as they could. They would never need to worry about being cold or hungry again.

How happy they were to hear their mother and father calling them through the forest. Their parents had been searching for the children from the day they had left them in the forest.

Laughing and crying, it was hard to believe they were all together.

"At last," said the woodcutter, "we can go home without any fears. We are a family again."

Sleeping Beauty

There was once a king and queen who seemed to have everything that anyone could possibly want. They had a lovely palace, huge estates, and all the people in the kingdom loved them. Yet, still they longed for just one thing more — a child of their own.

Then, after many a sad and lonely year, a baby daughter was born.

The king and queen were so happy.

"We shall give a party to celebrate," announced the king.

"And all the fairies shall be invited!" cried the queen.

So the invitations were written,
ready for birds to take them to all
parts of the kingdom. Nobody
saw one invitation fluttering down
into the lake . . . .

It was the invitation for the Fairy Carabos.
When she heard there was to be a royal party, and she was not invited, she was furious!

She ran to the palace, where the other fairies were gathered around the cradle, ready to bless the royal baby with gifts of kindness, happiness and beauty.

"Hah!" screamed a cruel, mocking voice. "Heed the spell of Carabos! On her fifteenth birthday, the princess will prick her finger on a spindle, and die!"

With a wild cackle of laughter
which rang all round the palace,
Carabos swept out, nodding her
head in satisfaction to hear the
gasps of horror behind her.

The fairies knew Carabos was far more powerful than them.

"But, perhaps," one said at last, "we can put our magic together and change the spell, just a little . . ."

"It means the princess will sleep for a hundred years when she pricks her finger," she told the king and queen. "But at least she will not die."

"All the spindles in the kingdom
must be broken!" cried the king.
"Then our child will be safe!"

Soon, the evil spell was forgotten. The princess grew beautiful, often dreaming of the handsome prince she hoped to marry, one day.

As the day of her fifteenth birthday approached, the king and queen planned the most splendid party. All the servants were very busy.

So the princess was left alone to
wander through the grounds by
herself. And that is how she came
across a little door she had never
seen before . . .

Soon, the princess was climbing a staircase which led to the very top of a high tower. There sat an old woman at a spinning wheel — something completely new to her...

"Come, learn to spin, my dear," cackled the old woman. "Just take the spindle . . ."

And in one terrible instant, the wicked spell of Carabos came true!

The beautiful young princess pricked her finger and fell to the ground. Very soon, even the wild, horrible screams of laughter from Carabos faded into complete silence.

Throughout the whole kingdom, nothing moved. The grass, the bushes and hedges around the palace grew tall and thick.

The story of the Sleeping Beauty became a legend, a tale which parents told their children. Until, one day, a brave prince decided to try and discover the truth . . .

On and on he rode, until he came to the forest, so thick and dark, there seemed no way in. But, as he raised his sword to cut through the greenery, a strange thing happened . . .

The forest of trees and bushes parted, so that he could lead his horse to the palace! Nothing had changed since the day when the evil spell of Carabos had come true . . .

The prince went through the little door and climbed the stairs. The last thing he expected to see was the princess, still young, still fast asleep . . .

She was so lovely, the prince
fell in love with her at once. As he
bent to kiss her, she opened her
eyes and gave him a sweet smile.

At the same moment, all the birds outside the window began singing, the leaves rustled in the breeze, and a bell sounded in the kitchen. The long sleep was over!

The prince had shown that love and courage could triumph over the worst evil! And the princess? She knew he was the sweetheart she had always dreamed of marrying, one day.